Arthur C James

Songs of Sixpenny and Pupilroom Pippings, etc

Arthur C James

Songs of Sixpenny and Pupilroom Pippings, etc

ISBN/EAN: 9783337020569

Printed in Europe, USA, Canada, Australia, Japan

Cover: Foto ©Andreas Hilbeck / pixelio.de

More available books at **www.hansebooks.com**

SONGS OF SIXPENNY

AND

PUPILROOM RIPPINGS,

ETC.

By ARTHUR C. JAMES.

R. INGALTON DRAKE,
ETON COLLEGE PRESS.

1899.

PREFACE.

THIS little collection has been strung together chiefly a
a personal parting gift to the members of my House
in the hope that it may serve to remind them of the lighter a
well as the graver side of one whose work among them has bee
a labour of love ; who has felt with them in all their cares and
successes ; and who hopes that in trying to do his duty to them
he has not unduly vexed them nor failed to win their regard.

A. C. J.

July, 1899.

SONGS OF SIXPENNY.

CRICKET.

Tɪɪs is "Second Edition." The First was shown up by my
old friend Philip Norman, the talented compiler of "Annals of
the West Kent Cricket Club," from which, by his special leave,
this is copied. It might therefore appropriately have appeared
as a "Pupil-room Ripping"; but the subject places it more
naturally as a "Song of Sixpenny," of which Club P. Norman
was Keeper. He has also most kindly allowed me to use the
Illustration, which is thought to represent either one or both of
the authors.

A T tennis, football, fives or golf
No prudent man would dare to scoff ;
But who can name another game
To hold its own with Cricket ?

For as we mingle in the strife
Which makes the sum of human life,
To small or great this mortal state
Recalls the well-laid wicket.

You'll sometimes find you must withstand
A man whose action's underhand—
Then keep your guard or else hit hard,
Nor deem 'tis wise to snick it.

Ere you play forward count the cost.
Then, he who hesitates is lost ;
Caught in the slips the weak one trips
    And must untimely kick it !

In politics, now in, now out,
One has to take one's turn about :
If you'd advance, ne'er miss a chance ;
    Hands low, and up you pick it !

Let each with prudence, skill, and nerve,
His side, not selfish interests, serve ;
Nor be cast down though Fortune frown,
    Whatever class your ticket.

But Life's a Ground that plays too fast,
The best long-hops are soonest past ;
The strongest player, the longest stayer
    Must sometime lose his wicket.

When work and sport alike are o'er
And the Great Umpire checks the score,
May we have won, not vainly run,
    Our life-long Game of Cricket !

LINES SUGGESTED BY THE ETON AND HARROW MATCH, ON AN EXPECTED TRANSFORMATION.

On G. B. Gosling's carrying his bat out after a fine uphill innings at Lord's, when a boy in jackets, July, 1889.

" Non usitata nec tenui ferar."—*Hor*. Od. II. 20.

BORNE on no usual or feeble quill
　　Through liquid air I'll steer ;
No more in Middle Club delaying still,
　　Heeding no envious sneer.

No village green for me !　Though known of yore
　　St. Mike's delight and pride,
I laugh at Michaelmas, hemmed in no more
　　By Chalvey's sluggish tide.

Already web-like pads my feet confine,
　　Buff plumage turns to white,
My hands smooth gauntlets don !　A Bird I shine,
　　In flannels snowy bright.

Soaring like him of Dædalean wing
　　I'll fly to echoing Lord's,
And even Australian grounds. a full-grown thing,
　　And Nott's northern swards.

The Quidnunc, and the house that scarce can blink
    Its dread of Radcliffe's team,
Shall learn my powers, and knowing youths that drink
    Ducker, and Itchen's stream.

O'er Gosling's wicket let no dirge be said :
    Fresh from defeat I rise.
Drop all that shrieking ! Gosling is not dead,
    Nor doomed to giblet pies !

TO THE BLACK CAT OF LORD'S.

—

July, 1894, when there was no playing weather on the
first day.

———————

BLACKER than clouds all yesterday which sat
    Pouring their pailfuls on the half-drowned rat,
Dyeing my linen through my sodden hat,
      Whence art thou, lordly cat?

Nought recking of those crowding eager faces,
Nor shouts of " Bowled " or " Played," with artful graces
Thou slimly slinkest through well-guarded spaces
      Where none but thou have places.

What? hast thou hopes of mice near this array?
No sparrows venture here.   See where they stray
Round luncheon tents to win what spoil they may,
      Out yonder, far away.

Here scarce a swallow skims the turf so neat,
Low, like the ball just driven past thy seat.
What omen thou, of victory or defeat,
      With fates so incomplete?

But, by Dame Sycorax, who rides the air
With thee her minion on her broomstick, spare,
—Hecat or she-cat, I nor know nor care,—
      Or rather, kindly square

Next year the elements, nor thus descend
With thy fell sisters and foul dogs, to end
In deluges the hopes of foe and friend
      Drowned in one miry blend !

So, when my garden-wall thou dost patrol,
May no glass points injure thy velvet sole,
No missile flower-pot or projected coal
      Down on thee carambole ;

But as upon the slates thou meet'st thy fair,
Thine alto be more killing for my prayer ;
And of thy nine lives, have just one to spare
      For that young batsman there !

BUTTON-HOLES.

Centaurea v. Myosotis.

LET others wear the curious Dendrobe,
    There comes not upon me a
Thirst to ransack the habitable globe
    And sport the rare Cattleya :

Unmoved I mark their not unconscious grace,
    As in diverse directions
Camellia-bosomed youths the Chapel pace,
    And countermarch by sections.

My modest verse shall praise two humbler flowers,
    One dark, the other lighter,
Of rival schools ; one where high Harrow towers,
    And one where Waynflete's mitre.

There dwelt a youth beside a lordly Hill,
    Where swallowtails are proper,
Where they play " footer " hard by " Ducker's " rill,
    And wear a straw for topper.

He was so wedded to the lore he knew,
    As if a rose were treason,
He made up button-holes of Harrow blue
    Throughout the cricket season.

One year he pined away, for Eton won :
    Whom Flora saw and pitied ;
Made him a cornflower ere his sand had run,
    And to her realm admitted.

He lived, he seeded, and the purpling corn
    Half won from scarlet poppies.
He shines at Lord's, by dark-eyed ladies worn,—
    Or, to speak sooth, his copies.

By Thames' brink a lowly flower appears,
    The turquoise-gem of Eton,
'Mid willow-weeds, wet with a river's tears,
    Whenever we are beaten.

Pensive it clings to memories that last,
    Though bright the cornflower's reign be,
Forget we not the glories of the past,
    The hopes that shall again be.

A request to Dr. Butler, Master of Trinity, for kind treatment and matriculation of *Foley*, who had got 100 against Harrow at Lord's, —and his answer! Foley was more successful at Trinity Hall, got into the University Eleven, and has been heard of elsewhere.

ILIAD, XXII. 345.

Τὸν δὲ κατηφήσας προσέφη Φωλεῖος ἀμύμων·
δάκρυ ἀναπρήσας, μάλα γὰρ κρατερῶς ἀπέειπε·
Ναὶ δὴ ταῦτά γε πάντα, ἄναξ, κατὰ μοῖραν ἔειπες·
ἀλλ' οὐ πάμπαν ἔφην ὑμᾶς τὰ μνησικακήσειν
οἵ ἔδρασα τὰ πρόσθε, σέθεν γ' ἀπόνοσφιν ἐόντος·
οὐδ' ἂν ἔγωγ' ἐθέλοιμι χολούμενος εἵνεκα νίκης
τῆσδε μαλ', ἣν πάθον ἄρτι, χόλον θυμαλγέα πέσσων
ἧσθαι ἐνὶ μεγάροις Ἰακώβου καλλικόμοιο·
οὔκ· ἔπει Ἡτῶνοι πολὺ φέρτεροι εὐχόμεθ' εἶναι
Ἀρροφίων, καὶ λᾶος ἀρηιφίλου Πτολεμαίου*.
ἀλλ' ἔκ τοι ἐρέω· ὡς καὶ τελέεσθαι οἴω·
ἔσσεται ἦμαρ, ὅτ' ἂν ποτ' ἐνὶ δνοφερῇ Λονδίνῃ
αὖθις δυσμενέεσσι πόνος καὶ δῆρις ὀρώρῃ.
πολλά τ' ἔσαντα πάραντα κάταντά τε δόχμιά τ' οἴω
παῖδας ἐφέψεσθαι κατὰ φράγματα ποιπνύοντας·
πόλλά τε κλαύσονταί γ' Εὐεργετέω* περὶ κρημνῷ
κοῦροι ἀτυζόμενοι παρὰ Φρείατος ἀγνὰ ῥέεθρα.
καὶ τότ' ἐγὼ μετέπειτα θεοῖς ῥέξας ἑκατόμβην,
γράψας τ' ἐν πίνακι πτυκτῷ θυμοφθόρα πολλά,
Εὐκλείδην τε καταστρέψας, (τοῦ γ' οὔτις ἀμείνων
ἑλκέμεναι νειοῖο βαθείης πηκτὸν ἄροτρον,)
ἐς Τροίην ἐπάνειμι γελῶν, δι' Ὀιοιο Γεφύρας,
πρὸς κλισίην Στάντωνος ἀρίφρονος· οὐδέ ἕ φημι
ῥηιδίως ἀρόσειν μ', εἰ νῦν γ' εὐήροτός εἰμι·
ἄλλο δὲ τοῦτ' ἐρέω· σὺ δ' ἐνὶ φρεσὶ βάλλεο σῇσιν·
Βόσπορος ἔστι πόλις,—καὶ Ἰωάννου πτολίεθρον,
θεσπέσιον, πολλοὶ δὲ σύες θαλέθοντες ἀλοιφῇ.
ἔστι τε Μαγδώλου πύργος, μεγά θ' ἕρκιον Αὐλῆς,
ἐν δὲ ἰῇ τιμῇ ἠμὲν κακὸς ἠδὲ καὶ ἐσθλός,

B

—ἐν δ' ἄροσις λείη· θεῖος δ' ὀρυμαγδὸς ὄρωρε.
πολλὰ δέ μοι ποτ' ἐφεῖτο πατὴρ καὶ πότνια μητὴρ
κεῖσ' ἀπιόντα μολεῖν—εἰ ταῦτ' ἀπο-Φώλια βάζεις.

* The names of the present Head Masters of Eton and Harrow may be expressed by the combined names of one of the Alexandrian kings.

Mercy—for *him* whose arm at Lord's so late
Cut, drove, and tipped " A Hundred " barbs of hate !
For *him* on whose detested head we fix
The guilt and shame of 1886 !
No ! *Mercy* let him crave at other knee,
Justice—no more—may he expect from me :
Justice,—yet tinged by Pity's mellowing hope
Poor Hector 'scape his feathered horoscope,
I trust he'll pass ; I would his wits were 'cuter ;
I've sent your letter to a σπλάγχνα-d Tutor.

H. M. B.

A DIRGE. (With apologies to Milton.)

When the "Monarch" was smashed in 1888, and went up on June 4th as two four-oars.

MOURN, Eton Muses, for a Monarch's fate :
    And thou, the tresses of thy waving weeds
Loosening, O Thames, with saltest tears of woe
Augment the Ocean's ceaseless ebb and flow ;
Our ruler leaves us in our sorest needs,
Our Upper Ten, our lordly Ship of State.
    But say, how chanced it ?   Fell he in the fray
Of battling ships on Eton's festal even,
When flags and plumes bedeck the proud array,
And smashing sculls in heaving locks are riven ?
Did hostile Prince, with his tumultuous crew
Press on the Victory and the Ten pursue,
While mad Defiance, rushing at thy realm,
Stove in thy stern and crashed upon thy helm ?
    Not so, ye Muses, for the month was May !
—Or did that noxious monster, breathing fire,
Behemoth erst, but later Steam-launch hight,
Roaring destroyer of each sweet delight,
Churning our river's reedy ooze to mire,
Loom unawares and plunge thee into night?
    Alas, what boots it with incessant care
To tend the homely oarsman's slighted trade,
And strictly meditate on training crews ?
Were in not better done as others use,
To trifle with lawn tennis in the shade,
Or cricket's coveted amusements share ?

Soft is the service of the felted ball,
Easy the flannels that the dry-bob earns,
Wickets are fresh and matches never pall,
These wring no hearts, their pleasure still returns.

Alas! No more with long and measured sweep,
With martial band-boats heralding thy way,
Shall Ampthill urge those timbers through the deep,
While punier Eights precede the proud array,
And to thy praise the echoing Brocas rings,
The last and longest of a line of Kings!

Silently now we draw thee to the shore,
Sadly look back upon thy twelve-years' reign;
Monarchs may live, and oar succeed to oar,
But not *our* Monarch, not our lordly Ten!

Eton Chronicle, June 4th, 1888.

ON A SWALLOW KILLED BY A GOLF-BALL.

O THOU poor little blithe swallow, unerringly
　　Darting after thy prey, now in aerial
Sport high under a cloud, now on a lower wing
　　　　Sweeping grassy declivities,

Be thy flight what it may, lost in entanglements,
Rush how wildly thou wilt, mazily tortuous,
Thee that moment awaits, dire, unavoidable,
　　　　That conjuncture particular,

That one point in the air, where with exactitude
Thou must meet with a ball urged by a golf-player,
All unconsciously driven, wildly coincident.
　　　　Now thou strugglest in agony!

Yet he, times out of ten, nine would have miss'd the ball,
Planted firmly to drive, still only topping it,
Who now standing aghast, sad and disconsolate,
　　　　Blames unthought-of obliquities.

Mourns that chance-driven stroke, aim unintentional.
Strange! who,—steel'd to destroy pheasants and partridges,
Nay, not seldomest known grimly to load again,
　　　　Scorning cries of a wounded hare,—

Sighs how nought it avail'd through the September hours,
Still to train for the flight, thee and thy little ones,
Sometimes lining the long wires of the telegraph,
　　　　Yearning aye for thy Southern home!

Thee no journey awaits now to Ausonia,
But through joyless abodes, realms Acherontian,
Must thou wearily flit, dreamily conscious of
       Imperceptible twitterings.

Yes, I'll carry thee home, wrapt in my handkerchief,
If perchance the rude blow prove not a mortal one.
E'en should desperate hope fail in thy hospitals,
       Blest in death, tho' unfortunate :

Since no tyrannous cat glared on thine agonies,
Rather tenderest hands strove to resuscitate,
And, if angels are not chanting thy requiem,
       Children sweetly lament thy doom.

PUPILROOM RIPPINGS.

— ⇒•⊏ —

THE DUFFER'S ALPHABET.

(From the "Grosvenor Guide to the Latin Prose Paper.")

A WITH an Ablative Agent expresses.
    B is the Bungler, whose Bungles one blesses.
C a 'Cui Quid' Verb, requiring, as 'dedit,'
D the poor Duffer, with Dative to wed it.
E is the Exercise ripped by his Tutor,
F the False Concords, as Feminine with Neuter.
G is the Gerundive misunderstood,
H is the Hash made of 'might,' 'would,' and 'should.'
I the Infinitive sadly misused,
J the Jobation which only confused.
    K is the Knowledge by this Book infused.
L the Light dawning on darkness so crass.
M are the Marks which now gain him a Class.
N are the Nouns he now makes to agree,
O his Oratio Obliqua with 'Se.'
P stands for Philoduff's Pride in his Prose,
Q for his 'Quods' and his 'Quums' and his 'Quo's.'
R is his Relative put indirect,
S his Subjunctive in Sequence correct.
T are the Trials in which he'll outshine all,
U is the Ut-clause in sentences Final :
    V is the Voice of his crow matutinal.
W the mark he now gets for his Beverley,
X the Exam. which he passes so cleverly.
Y is our Young friend a Duffer no more?
Z = the Answer : now find it and score.

A POOR Assistant Master at a Public School was spending a hard-earned Easter vacation at Florence, and with characteristic industry was looking through the treasures of the Medicean Library ; when he had the luck to light upon a MS. which had hitherto escaped notice.

After a very complete and satisfactory Collation, (the hospitality of the Library authorities is well known, and worthy of the representatives of Lorenzo the Magnificent), the MS. appeared to be a fragment of a second edition of some play of Aristophanes. The parallel case of the *Clouds* is well known. After removing the medieval nonsense which some monkish driveller had written above the text, interspersed with what appeared to be Illuminations in yellow and green Chartreuse, the text became fairly intelligible. The work evidently must be assigned to the Middle Comedy, as although individuals are referred to, the allusions are veiled, and no personal satire can have been intended, moreover the fragment certainly refers to a state of circumstances no longer existing.

PHILODUFF seated in school soliloquises. KRATEROLENOS, K.S. is seated opposite him : *Time*—11-35 *a.m.* on a Thursday in February, when Speeches are at 11-45.

ΦΙΛΟ. "Οσα δὴ δέδηγμαι τὴν ἐμαυτοῦ καρδίαν·
ἥσθην δὲ βαιὰ, πάνυ δὲ βαιὰ τέτταρα.
ἃ δ' ὠδυνήθην, ψαμμακοσιογάργαρα.
φέρ' ἴδω· τί δ' ἥσθην ἄξιον χαιρηδόνος ;
ἐγῷδ' ἐφ' ᾧ γε τὸ κέαρ εὐφράνθην ἐγώ.
Εὐκαρδίου τελέσαντος ἐς τοὺς μουσικοὺς

πάντως ἐγανώθην· ἄξιον γὰρ Καντάβροις.
Ἀλλ' ὠδυνήθεν ἕτερον ἀνθεμωτικόν·
ὁτὲ γὰρ κεχήνῃ προσδοκῶν Ἀνδήλιον,
ὁ δ' ἀνεῖπεν " εἴσαγ' ὦ Ἀηδὸν τὴν Κτίσιν,"
πῶς τοῦτ ἔσεισέ μου δοκεῖς τὴν καρδίαν ;
ἥσθην δὲ τῆτες, ὠνομασμένος τὸ πρὶν
Κορωνίδης¹ ὅτε προεγράφη Πολεμαρχίδης·
ὡς δ' εὐτυχῶς Βαρυβαῖος ἠγωνίζετο.
περυσὶ δ' ἀπέθανον καὶ διεστράφην ἰδὼν
ὅτ' ἀσφαλὴς ὁ Στύδδος ὢν ἐξεδράμῃ.²
ἀλλ' ἕτερον ἥσθην, ἡνίκ ἐπὶ τῇ Τεφράδι³
λάθρα παρακύψας ἔβλεπον Βαλλήναδε⁴
ὅπου 'καθῆθ' ὁ φαλακρὸς Ἱππαλεκτρύων,
πίλῳ δ' ἀρ' ἔπρεπε κρᾶτα περιβεβλημένος.
ἀλλ' οὐδεπώποτ' ἐξ ὅτου 'γὼ ῥύπτομαι
οὕτως ἐδήχθην ὑπὸ κονίας τὰς ὀφρῦς,
ὡς νῦν, ὁπότ' οὔσης κυρίας ἐκκλησίας
ἑωθινῆς ἔρημος αὑτηί σχολή.
οἱ δ' ἐν ἀγόρᾳ λαλοῦσιν οἱ διδάσκαλοι
γλώσσαισιν ἀτόποις Τευτονικαῖς καὶ Κελτικαῖς
περὶ πραγμάτων καὶ γραμμάτων καὶ σκηψέων,
δείπνων, γραφῶν, ὑπερημέρων, κλαυσουμένων,
νοσερῶν, ἀπόντων, δραμάτων Εὐριπίδου,
χαρτῶν ὑπωχρῶν, δυνάμεων, προβλημάτων,
κωπῶν θαλαμιῶν, Λαμάχου κηρυγμάτων.
οὐδ' οἱ νέοι γ' ἥκουσιν· ἀλλ' ἀωρίαν
ἥκοντες εἶτα γ' ὠστιοῦνται πῶς δοκεῖς
ἤδη παρόντες ἐσχάτων περὶ ξύλων,
ἄθροοι καταρρέοντες ; ἡ Σχολὴ δ' ὅπως
ἔσται προτιμῶσ' οὐδέν· ὦ πόλις πόλις.
ἐγὼ δ' ἀεὶ πρώτιστος ἐκ τῶν δωμάτων
νοστῶν κάθημαι· κᾆτ' ἐπειδὰν ὦ μόνος
στένω κέχηνα τίλλομαι λογίζομαι
ἀπορῶ γράφω τὴν κλεψύδραν ἔχων χερί.

(Enter the rest of the Division.)

’Αλλ’ οἱ μάθηται γ’ οὑτοιί μεσημβρινοί.
οὐκ ἠγόρευον ; τοῦτ’ ἐκεῖν’ οὑγὼ ’λεγον·—

’ΑΓΓΕΛΟΣ. "Ἄπαντες ἤδη πάριτε πρὸς τοὺς ῥήτορας.

Exeunt omnes

N O T A T Æ.

1. Cornicem illum significat poeta, qui agnomen Bellicum sibi vindicavit.

2. Verbum passivè dictum suspectum habet Dufferius, et satis absurdè ἐξέδραμεν legit.

3. Hæret in hoc loco Laticurvus noster homo perspicacissimus, qui Τετράδι interpretatur su
   periculo de quarto hebdomadis die. Ille autem erat " dies Cinerum " (Ash Wednesday)

4. *Cf.* Acharn, 204.

TWO EPIGRAMS OF SERTUM.

*A Ripping done for the Marquis of Graham, whose Translations,
when in Fourth Form, sometimes reached several editions.*

I.   No. 103 (ἀρθεὶς ἐκ Ζεφύρου πνοιῆς).

YOUNG Venning flew, blown by the Zephyr's laugh,
   Through ether, being lighter far than chaff.
And he'd have spun till Doomsday, but instead
He hung entangled by a spider's thread.
A week he hung suspended.   Then the spinner
Landed him safely, just in time for dinner.

II.   No. 104 (τέθνηκ' Εὐτυχίδης ὁ μελόγραφος).

So Pipes is gone! Ye shades of Pluto's cities,
Bolt all : for Pipes has got his " Nunc Dimittis."
And he has had cremated on the pyre, his
" Behold now Praise " and half a dozen Kyries :
Five scores of anthems, and his new Cantata,
Tedious " Te Deums," and a " Stabat Mater."
Where can we flee to now ?   The question dazes :
Since Pipes is made Precentor of St. Blaize's !

DEDICATION TO MY CLASS, OF A TRANSLATION OF THE PLUTUS, FOR MODERN READERS.

NOT to the riper scholar, but to those
    Who twice a week would round my table close,
Less fine in brain but of compacter thews,
Their lips to moisten with the Attic Muse,
Dreading the deep Pindaric Hippocrene,—
I give this draught, which like a vintner keen
I brewed for them, tapped as we went along,
And slily watered where it seemed too strong.

Oft on a summer's morning, fresh from Prayer,
We'd take our reading in the garden's air,
If no Shahzada wagged his dusky head,
Or gay Apostle dight in blue and red,
Or rare Smith's Prizeman made less holy bar,
Saint yet unnoted in the Calendar.

Five kindly youths, beneath the thorn-trees' shade,
One in the swing, one in the hammock swayed.
The rest in wicker chairs about the bower,
And those who best performed deserved a flower.
I deemed the liquor good and generous juice,
And worthy bottling off for future use.
Others must judge, transferred to modern times
Whether it smacks well in our northern climes,
This comedy, erst acted on the lees,
The latest play of Aristophanes.

DEDICATED TO THE SHINNER QUARTETTE
AND MISS LEHMANN, who sang "If thou
wilt be the honey-bee," &c.

IF thou wilt be the Honey-dew and burn in me alway,
   Then I will be the smooth white bowl formed of the Ocean
      spray.
If thou wilt be the smooth white bowl formed of the Ocean
      spray,
Then I will be the Amber stem and kiss thee all the day.

If I shall be the Amber stem and kiss thee all the day.
Then thou shalt be the bright ' Fix'd Star' of Bryant and of
      May.
If I shall be the bright ' Fix'd Star' of Bryant and of May,
Then thou shalt be the box, and I will light no other way.

Reminiscence of Shinner Concert, Windsor, Nov. 1888.

FROM THE GERMAN.   " Ich denke dein," &c.—*Goethe.*

I THINK of thee, when the Sun's earliest shimmer
          O'er sea is streaming :
I think of thee, when with the moonlight's glimmer
          Fountains are beaming :
I see thee, when above the distant highway
          Sand-storms are tossing,
In darksome night, when by some narrow by-way
          Wanderers are crossing.
I hear thee, when with deep reverberation
          The waves are leaping,
Listening in silent woods I take my station
          When all is sleeping.
I stand by thee and thou art still before me,
          Though space conceal thee.
The Sun sinks down, the stars are shining o'er me ;
          Might stars reveal thee !

———

Sung by Miss Lehmann at the same Concert.

FRAGMENTUM EX HOMERI HALIADE.

ASCHAMICIS

CENTESIMUM CONSESSUM CELEBRANTIBUS

EDIDIT

A. C. J.

Ὡς οἱ μὲν πονέοντο δέμας πυρὸς αἰθομένοιο,
τειρόμενοι πλεόνεσσι μαθήμασιν ἥπερ ἵσαντο,
Κελτῶν τ' Ἀργείων τε πολυκλαύτων τε Λατείνων,
ὀτρηροὶ θεράποντες ἀρίφρονος Ὁρμβοίοιο·
τειρομένοισι δ' ἔειπε μετ' Ἀσχαμίοισιν Ἰουδᾶς
Κήτειος· μικρὸς μὲν ἔην δέμας, ἀλλὰ μαχητής·
ἤρχετο δ' Ἰτώνεσσι μέγ' ἀφνειὸς βιότοιο,
τὸν δ' ἱερεὺς τέκετο μεγάροις ἔνι, μάντις ἀμύμων,
ὃς λαὸν ποίμαινεν ἐΰδμητον περὶ βωμόν—
ὅς σφιν εὐφρονέων ἀγορήσατο καὶ μετέειπε.
Δεῦτ' ἄγετ' Ἀσχαμίων ἡγήτορες ἠδὲ μέδοντες·
πὰρ γάρ μοι κλισίῃ μεγακήτεϊ νηὶ μελαίνῃ,
δεῖπνον ἐφοπλισόμεσθα, φίλοι, μετὰ μῶλον Ἄρηος·
ῥηιδίη δ' ἄνεσις λαοῦ ἀπονοστήσαντος.
Ὡς ἔφαθ'. οἱ δ' ἄρα πάντες ἐπῄνεον, οἳ ἀγόρευεν,
μῦθον ἀγασσάμενοι Κητείου ξανθικόμοιο·
ὀψὲ δὲ μύθων ἦρχε γέρων Ἄλιος [νημερτής].
Ὦ φίλοι, ἦ μάλα δὴ φίλου ἀνδρὸς ἐς ὑψερεφὲς δῶ
φήμ' ἴμεν· οὐ γὰρ ἔοικ' ἐπιδεύεσθαι παρεόντων.
πολλὰ δ' ἐν ὑψιπύλοισι δόμοις κειμήλια κεῖται
κέδρου τ' εὐκεάτοιο καὶ ἀργύρου ἠδ' ἐλέφαντος
χρύσεα τ' ἀμφικύπελλ'· ὁ δ' ἄρ' ἐν τρητοῖς λεχέεσσι
τέρπεται ἐν θαλίῃσι· ἅλις δ' οἴνοιο παρέσχε
κίπνου τ' ἀσβέστοιο· σέβας μ' ἔχει εἰσορόωντα.

εἴθ᾽ ὡς ἡβώοιμι, βίη δέ μοι ἔμπεδος εἴη
ὡς ὅτε πὰρ Κᾶμον—τί δὲ χρὴ μ᾽ ἀνεμώλια βάζειν ;
ἀνθ᾽ ὧν οὐκ ἂν ἔγωγε λιποίμην δαιτὸς ἐΐσης,
οὔτ᾽ ἐγὼ οὔτ᾽ Ἄρτουρος, ἐπεὶ κατὰ μοῖραν ἔειπες.

---

3. "Κελτῶν" de silicibus quisbusdam dictum putant nonnulli quas ex Thamesi trahendas curaverit Ἅλιος illa infra memoratus. Iidem "Ἀργείων" ad "argillaceous clay," "Λατείνων" ad "slate" referunt (cf. stlis = lis), vix autem credibile est Aschamicos in arte Geologicâ tantum profecisse. Κελτῶν ad linguam Gallicam potissimum referes.

6. Κήτειος, alii Κητείδης. Spartanus hic genere, quod satis liquet ex epitheto "Λακεδαίμονα κητώεσσαν." μαχητής, Angl. "Hit-tite." Hittitas vero (apud Ægyptios Khita, apud Homerum Κητείους, λ. 521), veteres Philistiae incolas a Joshua expugnatos testatur Gladstonius.

8. ἱέρευς. Sc. Episcopus, Judæ pater. Scriba quidam ad avum Keate, Βωμὸν ad "triste lignum," ubi victimas caedebat creberrimas (conf. Angl. "block-system") frustra conatus detorquere.

17. [νημερτής] sic tamen omnes fere Codd. Reddidit Pontifex noster—
         "Then slow uprose the venerable H*l*,
         Oracular in speech the truth to veil."

24. κάπνου. Mirabitur lector inter has luxuriae delicias fumi etiam mentionem fieri. Hinc autem pro certo habeo hoc fragmentum Homero dandum esse, qui et Ulyssi fumum admodum arrisisse testatur—
         "ἱέμενος καὶ κάπνον ἀναθρώσκοντα νοῆσαι."

28. Ἄρτουρος. Recte pro amico suo Jacobo Minore respondet senex, apud quem ille inter æquales puer artem mathematicam didicisse dicitur, sicut apud Chironem Achilles.

SONG OF THE TARDY.

OF all books I've done since Eton first mother'd me,
   " Thick-sides " and thin sides, in cloth and in boards,
There's one book which more than all others has bother'd me,
   And there are no cribs and no " word-for-words."

     For near the School-yard a book
     Lies, 'tis the Tardy-book,
     Thither I'm hurried before I'm awake ;
     Yes, 'tis the Tardy-book,
     Never a harder book
     Loomed in the window of Williams or Drake.

When I first came to Eton how gaily I'd hurry up,
   Soon after seven when Gilder came round,
Lace up my boots before locking my burry up
   'Ere the half-hour through the dark could resound.

     How strange and ill-starred a book,
     Then seemed the Tardy-book :
     Now how it haunts me before I'm awake.
     Bother that Tardy-book !
     Never a harder book
     Frowned from the shop-front of Williams or Drake.

But now 'tis my object to have my last slumber out,
   Slip my great-coat on and pumps if I'm late,
Splash through the mud to the Office I lumber out,
   Back into bed then till twenty to eight,

Having done that old Tardy-book,
Blotted and marred a book
Doomed 'ere to-morrow deep vengeance to take ;
Bother that Tardy-book,
Never a harder book
Banged on the counter of Williams or Drake.

Palinode.

Meantime Rhadamanthus and Minos and Æacus,
  Crouch in their dark and malodorous bower,
Nought recks honest Gaffney, nor cares the Fusee a cuss,
  Though but two seconds it's gone the half-hour !
    Ah ! bring back the Tardy-book !
    Why fiercely guard a book
    Where we're so anxious our names should appear ?
    For Bradley's a harder book,
    And of Milton the Bard a book,
    With interest compound, if paid in arrear.

OBED.

ETONA'S towers to mortal gaze,
 Lit by the sun's declining rays,
  Assume a greyish hue—
And Eton's sons on study bent,
On verses and on prose intent,
  Now work till all is blue.
Hark! from a form in " No. eight"
A cry is raised, " As sure as fate
  My Tutor's is on fire!"
" What? where?" ejaculates the Beak,
" Who was the boy that dared to speak
  And brave my righteous ire?"
" Look, sir, yourself." " By Jove! 'tis true!
Quick, every mother's son of you!
Run, call the engines! hurry! do!
  No time to lose, I say!"
No need the order to repeat,
The boys were all upon their feet,
And scampering up the neighbouring street
  To mingle in the fray.
Tell, Muse, who then, outstepping all
With nimble foot, was first to call
  The Eton Fire Brigade.
He who as " Ginger "'s known to boys,
A foe to peace, a friend to noise
  And ballyragging raid.

Scouring the street he knows so well,
His hand is first to ring the bell,
And quick responding to the knell
    The Firemen rush to arms—
With hatchet, helmet, badge and belt,
Down through the crowded street they pelt ;
No timorous qualm of fear they felt,
    Inured to Fire's alarms.
Just then, they say, that driving by,
Great England's Royal Majesty,
Scanning the glowing western sky,
    The flames beheld afar.
And clasping the Princess's arm,
Exclaimed in accents of alarm,
" Now Heaven in mercy shield from harm
    That true and faithful Gar ! "
Gar ! who ere then had quenched the flames
Threatening with ruin Arthur James !
Gar, first and foremost of all Dames
    When danger's in the air—
She summons all her trusty aids,
Boy's—Kitchen—Parlour—Scullery maids,
" All to the rescue quick ! ye jades !
    No fear when I am there !"
" Why, ma'am ! now don't ye call us names,"
Says one emerging from the flames,
    " We've done our level best ; "
And shortly to the startled gaze,
With eyebrow scorched and cap ablaze,
The heroine of former days.
    Bold WICKENS stands confessed.

For as our *Chronicle* has shown,
(What testimony higher?)
Bold Wickens long ere this had known
 The Baptism of Fire.
" Fly, bring the cans and waterjugs,
Milk, beer, whatever's handy, rugs
 To quench the nascent flame."
Stirred by her voice they work like blazes,
Soon naught remains to meet our gazes
 But smoke, and dirt and—FAME!
Yes, Fame for " GAR "—who sought no aid
From engine, hose or fire brigade—
And like one other far-famed Maid
 Has won a peerless name.
" Three cheers for ' GAR ;' for she's the man,"
The little urchins shout ;
At half past five the fire began,
 At six the fire was out.

       F. TARVER.

ETON BACHELORS' ASSURANCE AND WEDDING PRESENT COMPANY, LIMITED.

PROSPECTUS.

THE Economics of Social Science have recently much engaged the attention of the British Association and other learned bodies.

In view of events imminent in our own Society, the uncertainty of Bachelor life at Eton seems to challenge particular attention.

It is the duty of every prudent man to set his own house in order, and on certain occasions it is his privilege to assist in doing the same to the houses of others. " Scimus, et hanc veniam petimusque damusque vicissim." So far all is as it should be. A proverb, however, tells us " It never rains but it pours ; " we are very liable to Floods at Eton, and as the days of Noe are associated with various phenomena, it behoves us before the glass falls to make due provision against rainy days, and, if possible, to equalise the rainfall and avoid waste.

It is proposed, therefore, to start a Company under the direction of some of our ablest financiers, to be intituled the " ETON BATCHELORS' ASSURANCE AND WEDDING PRESENT COMPANY, LIMITED."

The objects of this Company will be twofold :—

    1. *(a)* To provide Bachelors with due Assurance.
    2.   To supply Wedding Presents for a fixed yearly subscription.

I.

The figures and details of this part of the Scheme have not yet been completely worked out, but are engrossing the attention of our most experienced Mathematicians. The main lines are as follows :—

It is proposed that each Bachelor who wishes for a Policy of Assurance shall pay a yearly premium, varying according to his Estimated Prospect of Celibacy : entitling him to receive Wedding Presents in the case of any fatal Accident.

The Premiums will be arranged in an ascending scale.

Class A. (paying the smallest premium) Fellows of King's College, Cambridge, under the old System.

Class B. Masters entitled to Pensions according to the Regulations of the Governing Body.

Class C. Masters not otherwise classified.

Class D. Masters who have taken a House within a year, or who stand next on the list, or who are considered to possess exceptional personal attractions.

Class E. Masters who go to Switzerland or Norway, or such countries where, ascents to higher ground being frequent, and the percentage of Accidents unusually high, the ascending scale also naturally culminates. These may maintain a Policy by paying a due deposit of Caution money to the Company. (They are recommended to invest in the Company's new Alpen Stocks, in case of any Settlement.)

Married Masters and Ladies to be entitled to belong to the Company on payment of a moiety of the premium of Class A.

II.

The advantages to the Donor, which will be secured by the Company, need scarcely be pointed out ; they embrace the following :—

(1) Avoidance of all trouble in buying Wedding Presents, which will be purchased by a Committee of Taste,

including persons of the highest practical and æsthetic talent.

(2) Total freedom from responsibility as to selection, as a Committee can always be abused without rudeness.

(3) Facilities for arranging combined presents.

(4) An unfailing topic for conversation at dinner admitting comparisons out of taste under the presen system.

The advantages to the Consumer will be equally obvious embracing

(1) Avoidance of confusion from variety of heterogeneou styles in plate, china, furniture, &c.

(2) Facilities for delicate intimation of desiderata.

(3) And of desideranda.

(4) Avoidance of duplicates.

(5) Where this is not possible, opportunity of re-sale to the Company at a moderate reduction.

It may be confidently expected that the Capital of the Company will be eventually augmented by a liberal grant from the Governing Body.

It is to be hoped that the Lower Master will accept the office of Chairman.

Purveyors to the Company, Herbert's Eton Stores.

Expected Capital, £20,000 in shares of £5 each. Applicant for Shares are invited to refer to A. C. BENSON, Esq., before the Greek Kalends of January, 1889.

Every offer, tender or otherwise, will be carefully considered and if eligible accepted.

N.B.—*Preference Shares are already at a premium.*

THE COMPANY'S OFFICE, ETON, 1888.

THE *AMPHIBIAN*, 1898.

O PAGE, be sponsor to our high intent!
  We long to make a bold experiment;
—Evolve a new superior race of Man,
Soon to be known as the *Amphibian.*
Why not? What boots it, all exempt from law,
To galvanize the throbbing frog's hind-paw,
Unwhipt of Justice in Division III.,
And letting Virgil Repetition be—
Unless we can develope some new breed,
And go one better on old Darwin's lead?
    There was an Age, 'twas Pliocene, they say,
When Earth was wetter e'en than this year's May.
O'er boundless waste roamed many a wondrous brute,
—Sad waste indeed, with no one there to shoot!
The muscular developement was great,
Each species struggling to some higher state;
Each kind did all it could, lived, fought, and wived,
And yet 'tis strange, the few alone survived.
They tried all elements, earth, water, air,
But education seems to have been rare;
Though Pterodactyls marked along the sand
Strange feet, by unborn races to be scanned.
Greeks were not yet; therefore no Tug of War
'Twixt Dinotherium and Plesiosaur!
    Not that we'd fain restore Primeval Man,
That were reaction : we would lead the van.
But lest our powers should grow too cribbed, confined,
We'd advocate a more amphibious mind.

E

For are we not too highly specialized ?
Each one exactly does as advertised.
" Take Carter's Liver Pills !   But be precise,
" Be sure they're Carter's, and say ' Carter's ' twice."
    'Tis thus the Amalgamated Smiths reprove
The hand that dares to work beyond his groove.
You'd think some fierce Trades Union pulled the wires,
Stinting our output, damping down our fires,
Refusing all amendments to permit.
Still making joiners join and fitters fit.
With us the fault exists but not the cause,
For we've not got to work with Labour Laws !
    Jones minor, Crichton of his private school,
Takes to the river or the bat by rule.
As soon as he has passed, the aspiring oar
Abjures the cricket field he loved of yore,
And now would rather sap all after six
Than take his spell at bowling at the sticks ;
Although the fresh departure made this year
In Junior Matches, may be useful here.
    Nor deem Aquatics wholly are to blame :
With other interests 'tis just the same.
Mark how the aspirant to " his Sixpenny "
Turns hydrophobe, lest bathing spoil his eye :
Scales the School List, and as he climbing pants,
Captains his Tutor's column of Non-Nants !
And yet, at Lord's, if sound of wind and limb,
He'd not play worse for having learnt to swim :
And no success in any athletic strife
Makes up for a lost chance of saving life.
    We need not wholly swallow all they say
Of those old worthies of primeval day,

When you might go from Newcastle to Devon
To find a man who'd *not* been in the Eleven ;
And all the Twenty-two were in the Eight !
Still there are some, not toothless up to date,
Who reached a foremost place by flood and land,
And thumbed their Classics with judicious hand.
For nothing harms a sound boy in his teens
Save apathy.   Learn that from the Marines !
That glorious body, fit for anything,
To rescue Britons or to sack a king,
Though few their medals and though short their pay,
—Think, who are so amphibious as they ?
Who loves a game of cricket like poor Jack,
Slewing off-balls round on the larboard tack ?
Long may he chase the ball at Wei-hai-Wei,
While Henry's mailéd fist applauds admiringly !
Nor less delight, on Summer after Four,
To mark our Guardsmen ply the unskilful oar,
When Independent firing from the bow
Commences, heedless of the coxswain's " Now ! "
Like a machine they'll march the breach to storm,
But in a boat—they drop the uniform !
   Well, old Etonians harp on the old tune,
Especially upon the Fourth of June.
For in no school's " laudator temporis
" Acti se puero " stronger than in this.
" What, can this *really* be ? " cried one of late,—
" In *my* days Pop existed for·debate !
" Why, this must make our statesmen of renown
" Turn in their Abbey, and their marble frown ! "*

* This refers to a state of things now happily reformed.

We must confess there's something in such jeers :
Pop's a survival, like Man's folded ears,
Still, we have many now, where there was one :
And Mind's put in commission, 'tis not gone.
All things are prone to change, they rise and fall :
Nothing stands still, and Eton least of all.
So most men, as they look around, can see
Shoots that are bettering the parent tree,
Something lopped off which did no good, or worse ;
More grafted in, to which they're not averse.
So still their sons they send, to work, or sock,
Chips of—and sometimes to—the same old Block,
Right glad to see them, tried by any test,
Not better than their fathers, but more blest.
Thus, by " Amphibian," pray don't understand
" What dies in water and can't live on land."
'Tis given to a few in one thing to excel,
But most can manage many fairly well.
This helps one at a pinch to help a friend,
And gives most satisfaction in the end.

PERSONAL AND DOMESTIC.

"CORNISH."

*A Serenade to the Future Vice-Provost of Eton, 1893. Sung
by a select band of friends, as set to solemn music by
A. M. Goodhart.*

" Fortunate senex ! Ergo tua rura manebunt !"...
" Nos patriae finis et dulcia linquimus arva,
" Nos patriam fugimus."

Virgil, Ecl. 1.

ACCEPT, dear Friend, the tribute that we raise,
While still thy comrades, to enhance the bays
Which soon shall crown that intellectual brow,
Fringed by soft curls of flax dissembling snow.

Achieved the honours of an useful life,
Mark time, while we prolong the fretful strife :
No longer thine to curb the fruitless spleen,
Nor start amazed from sleep at seven-fifteen.

Sound as yon pigeons roost with muffled heads,
Heedless of cats which steal along the leads,
Though nearer now the College bell may hang,
Sleep deep beneath its unregarded clang.

But hark! With ponderous bolt and massy bar
Janus admits Reduplicated Warre![1]
From cloistered tower great Edmond greets a friend,
And martial names resound from end to end.

Receive, ye solemn and monastic cells,
Gladstonian statesmen and æsthetic belles,
While sainted Henry[2] smiles benignantly
On reverend forms of Harcourt and O. B.,

Whose Chief, grown harmless in extreme old age,
Shall scan Home Rule[3] in the Mæonian page,
New projects for unUlstered Irelands weave,
And grant the British Empire a reprieve.

I see the salons of a cultured dame
Surpass the gatherings of Parisian fame,
Where Oliphants and Sidgwicks and de Staëls
Vie with our ever-memorable Hales.

Safe in the Library from noontide heat,
How sweet you'll find old Wotton's calm retreat,
As from old shelves the antique and dusty Muse
Pours forth her treasures into new Reviews.

Nor let thy genius smoulder all unseen;
Hand the bright torch, and fire the Magazine!
Nor tremble weakly on Creation's verge,[4]
Beyond it dare thy Pegasus to urge!

Anon while we still ply the ungrateful part,
Resume as erst old Izaak Walton's Art,
Lure Thames' chub to seize the whirling flies,
Should Thames' trout not to the occasion rise.

Thus may'st thou thrive the Unpensioned to impress,
Thy fame commanding,—nor thy shadow less!
Fat grow thy Frame to fit thine ample stall,
—And point an Article by Kegan Paul!

---

1. The "Duplex bellum" of Livy.
   Also compare Homer, II. v. 31
   Ἄρες Ἄρές βροτολοιγέ, μιαιφόνε, τειχεσιπλῆτα,
   and Æsch. Ag. 643. δίλυγχον Ἄτην, φοινίαν ξυνωρίδα.

2. Not Henry of Northampton, but Henry of Lancaster.

3. Scan it thus :
   "Quot mala diviso moliris, *Homerule*, regno."

R. C. J.

4. "There are times when he appears to tremble on the verge of creation."

S. H. B.

SONNET TO MISS IONA R.

With a copy of " Ionica."

NOT from those violet isles of Western Greece,
　　Nor from the statelier cities which of yore
Looked into sunset from the Ægean shore
O'er varied tracks of bay and Chersonese,
Home of the Muse whose grace shall never cease ;—
But from the Northern island which upbore
Columba's cross our Britain to explore,
Fit stepping-stone for harbinger of peace,
Apt god-mother for lives of pure content,
Was born the inspiration of thy name.
And this I deem a source more excellent
Than what Greek origin this book may claim.
Ionian airs may charm a leisure hour,
But Northern breezes give the life its power.

COLLEGÆ ÆQUÆVO. S. P. D. A. C. J.

In quinquagesimum aetatis annum.

FRIEND of my youth, my manhood's pride,
    Whom sluggards fear and fools deride,
What birthday offering shall be given
To Twenty-six from Twenty-seven?
—Not years, but days, of February—
In honour of your Jubilee?
Congratulations on the past,
And hopes for blessings that may last.
Grudge not the snows that thicklier patch
That comely and Luxmooriant thatch,
Nor that you now less deftly stoop
To cheat the fives-ball's skimming swoop!
Still be it yours to wrap up truth
In cobwebs of Ruskinian sooth :
Hand on the lamp, and by it toil
With more of Light, if less of Oil.
Stipple the sky, and plant the tree,
And delve the ground right heartily,
Nor, e'en when Sixty's drawing nigh,
Look back to Forty with a sigh.
Use thus your life, till it grow dark,
And Sexton shall inter our Clerk.

a.d. Kal. Mart. IV.
A.S. MDCCCXCI.

P

AD COLLEGAM ÆQUÆVUM.—FEB. 28TH.

FRIEND, whose adventure on this Earth
    Succeeded mine by one day's birth,
Thanks to your flock, for blossoms sweet
Which made my morning school a treat !
These snowdrops felt no hireling's hand,
Those violets ne'er saw Scilly's strand,
But scents from your own bowers bring,
Where Winter steals the rays of Spring,
And creepers bar to entrance vile
The Poet's Corner of our Pile !

Each time I greet an added year,
I ask, " How long abide we here ?
" Will my bare head sink first from sight,
" Or yours, more picturesquely white ? "
I know not.   In a lifelong way,
Small is the vantage of a day,
This matters little, but we'll own,
'Tis good not to have run alone.

Etonae, pridie Kal : Mart :
    MDCCCXCVII.

ON THE BIRTH OF MY ELDEST GRANDSON, AND THE NAMING THEREOF, WHICH WAS A MATTER OF GREAT UNCERTAINTY.

A N old and sympathetic Pair
 Achieved their first-born son,
But when they came to choose a name,
 'Twas easier said than done.

Kinsfolk and family and friends
 Climbed up the Family Tree :
What made things worse was that the Child
 Was one of Destiny.

The Sire his counsel kept perforce,
 Locked up in his own pate ;
For he was dumb, and therefore took
 No part in the debate.

And ' Zachariah,' ' Barachiah,'
 He looked on these with dread :
And when, perplexed, they mounted higher,
 He sadly shook his head.

And as to speak he was not able,
 He put off every one
By asking for a writing-table,
 And wrote, " His name is John."

And writing thus, the good old man,
 He straightway found his tongue,
Gave praise to Heaven, nor only that,
 But burst out into song.

The child was named, the child was nursed,
　　He fought the fight and won.
Others, at Sulham and elsewhere,
　　Were after him called John.

At Newcastle, at Osborne Road,
　　Next door to ninety-one,
There is a writing-table fine,
　　A gift from brother John. .

' Andrew Brunel Marc Armstrong Giels,'
　　The list seems rather long ;
If ' Coleridge Parsifal ' you add,
　　It makes it still more strong.

You, father, cut the knot, and say
　　" An ounce is worth a ton."
The table stands there : either write
　　Or speak, " His name is John."

May, 1892.

TO A LADY.

With a birthday gift especially asked for—maggots for her
Virginia nightingale ; also a song by Tosti.

B E thine, dear Friend, with due returnings
Of birthdays, all life's choicest earnings.
Accept herewith my gifts symbolic,
All in regard, if part in frolic.
Not as gifts once were sent to bring
A menace to the Persian king,
Bird, Scythian arrows, frog and mouse,
—A problem worthy Mr. Rouse.—
Lest mine should keep your nerves in tension,
I will expound my quaint invention.

I sat at Venice late, *cinmal*,
One evening, by the Grand Canal,
Smoking my pipe, in my great coat,
Pleased at out-living *table d'hôte*,
But tired of waiting, like a draper,
Till Mr. Mozley 'd read the paper.
The stars were bright.   The crescent moon
Mirrored herself in the lagoon :
Sunset's last rays had done their duty
On the scrolled domes of the Salute.

A gondola drew near.   Uprights
Suspended Chinese lantern-lights ;
Whence came such strains as Southern throats
Emit when bent on lira notes.

The timbrous tenors strove to show
Their too continuous tremulo,
Yet all in tune harmonious blending,
Though wanting in diminuending.
The double-bass, the flute and viol,
Support the amorous descant's trial.

This ceased.   Then after brief repose
A female voice as sweet uprose,
As which by Serbellonian billow
Chased sleep from the Luxmoorian pillow.
Or as the dark-haired choir-boy rises
Upon some breathless anthem's crisis,
To sing, on week-days, strains that *you* know,
Of Barnby, Sullivan or Gounod,
Or sweetlier, (if not too coldy,)
" Dove's wings " by Mendelssohn Bartholdy,
Or, —should the Provost be at prayers,
On Sunday morn, —perhaps by Nares.
I listened rapt.   Then nearer drew
The gondola, and I bent to view,
Thinking of Philomel, or Procne,
If " Philomel " perchance, is cockney.

I saw ; yet saw no lovely maid,
But old, and plain, and meanly clad.
She seemed all voice, which sweetly rang :
(I thought I'd send you what she sang.)
More like to our plain British bird
Which oft from nightly bush is heard,
Than to Virginia's plumage gay
Which on your terrace gives no lay.

Yet try the cage, that separate bowers
May stimulate the dormant powers.
Next, send I mealworms for their meat :—
Without a meal what voice is sweet ?

These are my gifts, both rare and good :
Symbolic, but when understood
As plain as Daniel read by Reuss,
Or preached by plainer Mr. Haweis.
And if my lay too long should be,
'Tis all the fault of your strong tea.

TO C. H. EVERARD,

From Pupil-room, on being asked to dinner to meet a
foreign company, and talk French.

DEAR Charlie, at your table be
    All joyousness and jollity.
Let guests be worthy fork and knife,
And sister vie in grace with wife.
But when you Gallicise the heights
Of conversational delights,
My Spouse it is, not I, may share
Proclivities to such high fare.
And as my fitter half's away,
I should prefer another lay,
And seek the warbling of the lute
Within the Albert Institute.
Unused to a Parisian Salon
I will not risk " essais de ballon."
At " parlez-vous " I'm not first-rate,
So wont aspire to your Banck-quête,
Putting prohibitive embargo
On poor John Bull's more homely cargo.

SENT WITH SOME MODELLING CLAY TO DR. BUTCHER, HOMŒOPATHIC PHYSICIAN.

DEAR Doctor, once you told me sadly
    One thing you wanted very badly—
A Body,—but your strict profession
Denied you flatly all possession.
Well, now I send you one,—myself :
Done with, and laid upon the shelf.
Cut, lance, trepan, dissect your fill,
And amputate it at your will.
" What's this ? a lump of earth," you say.
Well, what is mortal man but clay ;
When soul has left him, food for worms,
Convertible to other forms ?
And if this clay should yet revive,
Taught by your plastic art to live,
In this it typifies its owner,
With the best wishes of the Donor.

TO F. A. J.
On her birthday.

PONCIE, thy loving joyous way,
    Grown something grave of late,
Makes me almost regret the day
    That brings thy years to eight.

For as these pass, there's something lost
    Which seems to taste of heaven,
As if some magic line we crossed,
    Untouched while we were seven.

Yet may such springtide long be thine,
    Nor, till experience brings
Both human strength and power divine,
    Put away childish things.

May 22, 1890.

TO A YOUNG LADY,

On her giving up Dolls.

DEAR Child, do not disdain your toys.
    What would we elder people give
Not to have quite outgrown your joys?
    Like you to think, like you to live?

Well used, the light of childhood's day,
    —The theme of many a sadder song,—
Will cast o'er life a sweetening ray,
    When hair is up and skirts are long.

Dig out your childhood's richest ore,
    Thence shall a thread of purer gold
Run by your path, and furthermore
    Direct the new life through the old.

Let Fred lie in his drawer apart,
    But when there's no one by to see,
Give him a corner of your heart,
    And sometimes look at him for me.

Nov. 6th, 1897.

" TUBEROSE."

CHARADE.

M Y first conducts o'er Father's soul
Soft balm from the Virginian bowl,
When by Joe Taylor's strictures mild
He's been unusually riled,

'Tis also noticed to combine
With Mr. Daman's bold sky-line,
And pleasingly to intersect
Those walls which Radcliffe's house protect.

My second blooms in many a nook
Among the vales of Willow-brook,
And quenches its own rootlet's thirst
By scattering water from my first.

My whole's a flower as sweet in scent,
With which one may be well content,
Though it has nought to do, 'tis reckoned,
Or with my first, or with my second.

But after all, what does this matter?
Gardeners are always on the smatter,
Make it three syllables, and see
If that will solve the mystery!

TO A YOUNG LADY,

On her Confirmation.

MY friends' dear child, my children's friend,
    'Tis sad your spring-time's hour should end ;
Your head episcopally blessed
By pendant tail no more be tressed ;
More sad, that Eton's lawns and bowers
Should yield thee to Treworgan's towers.
Yet tend your dormice, six or seven,
And feel yourself the nearer Heaven.
At wall-eyed " Prince's "* foibles laugh,
And wean him from my fatted calf !
And as you grow more round of line,
And " Winnie's " merged in " Catherine,"
Though we no longer see you here
Demurely pace Keate's Lane with " Dear,"
Still may your Nature grow in grace,
Your soul reflect your Mother's face !

       * A rather spoilt dog which had bitten the writer.

Eton, Easter, 1895.

WITH A SILVER SHIP,

To Mr. & Mrs. J. Carter, (late for their Silver Wedding).

SLOOP, Galleon, Caravel, or Amiral,
     With spars all taut and bellying sails withal,
I come, three years belated at the least,
Missing, alas! your silver wedding-feast :
Quite given up at Lloyd's, long overdue,
Assurance paid, of Life and Friendship too.
Well, let's renew the same old Policy,
This underwriter asks no second fee!

On many a tack I've sailed the world around,
Last from Port Arthur am I homeward bound ;
Soon may your children climb each silver cord,
And board my deck, the while I deck your board.
There I'll admire your choicest Japanese,
Your dinners, your Consolidated Teas,
Your jewelled glass from Venice or from Prague,
Your wares from Whiteley's, panels from the Hague.
Watch fleets of buxom beakers, pint and quart,
Salute my pennant as you pass the Port.
Then, when you've settled Jem and Jack and Tom,
And leave the Timbralls, nevermore to roam,
Tow me to moorings safe, and say, " Our Ship comes home!"

To Mr. and Mrs. W. A. CARTER,
On their Golden Wedding-Day.

" DONAREM PATERAS......BURSARINE."

UPON your festive board I'd gladly lay
    Apt presents for your golden wedding-day :
Gifts meet to grace, in metal and in size,
Well-auspicated quinquagenaries.
But ah ! I can't afford such things, for we
Have been cut down so by the Governing B. !

Yet be your age as golden as your prime ;
Rich with the hues of mellow sunset-time !
Garnered with sheaves meet for the eternal store,
Together may you reach that threshing-floor !

We bow to you and pensive take our way :
For masters come and go, but Carters stay.
Then gazing on such strength, your juniors cry
" κεκαρτέρηται τἀμά," ere we die.

July 31st, 1895.

INSCRIBED IN A COPY OF THE ILLUSTRATEI EDITION OF GREEN'S "SHORTER HISTORY OI THE ENGLISH PEOPLE."

Sent as a Wedding Present to a Young Lady of deep reading and of solid tastes in books.

FAIR fugitive from lordly halls,
    From pines and oaks umbrageous,
Nurtured in scenes whose beauty palls,.
    Yet haply was contagious.

Though Herbert Spencer and though Mill
    Supply thy lightest reading,
With stronger meat, which might make ill
    Maids of less wholesome breeding,

Though Ruskin seems to thy calm mind
    Nought but a wild alarmist,
And Tennyson a bard confined,
    —A very sorry psalmist.

Yet think, Great Gladstone oft unbends
    In eloquence convivial,
And through the Post-card condescends
    To things extremely trivial ;

Darwin, evolving Man from snails,
    Wrote of the earthworm's habits;
Hunters who follow tiger's trails
    Deign to seek sport with rabbits !

Then take this book.   Slight work like Green's
  May not escape thy strictures,
Yet future Lilians in their teens
  Some day will love the pictures ;

And with these volumes take this verse,
  Fair cousin, with my benison :
You'll say, " It could not well be worse,
  " But still,—he is not Tennyson ! "

December 11th, 1893.

SONNET,

With a Drawing of Segesta in Sicily.

WHAT ancient memories yon stones recall!
  That is Segesta : whose unreal state
And promised wealth, and show of borrowed plate,
Tempted the vain Athenians to their fall.
Look at the grandeur of those pillars tall,
Though limned by hand of skill inadequate.
For six-and-twenty centuries those great
Columnar masses have been reared : yet all
Unfinished : wanting still the enrichment due
Of fluted lines from capital to base.
Ere that could be, swooped down upon the place
With ruthless sword Agathocles, and slew
Ten thousand men, and Grecian ladies knew
What slavery meant with a barbarian race.

HOLYDAYS.

—➤•◄—

TO THE SECRETARY OF THE ASCHAM SOCIETY,

In answer to an invitation to dinner, upon his resignation of
the office, Dec. 1887.

IN care and sorrow closes in the year!
　　The shortening days now give us counsel sere.
December warns us of the old poet's sign,
How we have slain the months, old Helios' kine.
As in change coats we pace the altered street,
We think of homes that happy faces greet.
Who roves abroad may vary but his sky ;
Who stays at home can only change his tie.
Yet ere, as unemployed, we line the square,
Our Working Men's Club throngs the thoroughfare.
Our Secretary, of all chiefs the best,
Requires attendance for the dinner-test.
As ever, to this last behest I bow,
But never half so willingly as now.
Of rulers thus he stands apart from all :
Never more popular than in his fall.
And bidden to partake of his good cheer,
We ask no turtle, either thick or clear :
For he who's fain from office high to stoop,
Fitlier regales his friend with Grévy-soup.

FOR THE VISITORS' BOOK, SIDBURY MANOR
DEVON.—Sept., 1895.

O HAPPY vale, O blest retreat,
 Where all but your champagne is sweet !
Where Nature vies with art, and old
Alcinous' glories are retold.
Oranges of Hesperian fruit
Grow golden on each Edith's shoot,
And never thorn, one might suppose,
Could lurk beneath that Banksia rose.
Can I forget those flowers rare,
Those tapestries of maiden-hair,
The morning plunge from grassy brink,
The long, long, tramp, the longer drink ?
Harboured in such abodes of bliss,
I think I'd like a place like this.
Here could I dwell, and ask no more,
But oh ! those "goyles "* at 54 !

* Hillsides of immense height, which one is expected to walk up and down for partridges.

TOTSIE LEWIS.

A holyday adventure at Malvern, 1897.

THEY came on bicycle and brake
  Along old Malvern's mountain bends,
A joyous holyday to take,
  Friends' children, and our children's friends.

We missed, we found, we hid, we sought,
  All cares thrown off, and books disused;
We wove adventures out of nought,
  By childhood's magic charm transfused.

Then in the cool secluded lake
  Each merry Naiad leaps and swims,
Till Dian's waves with laughter shake,
  Dimpling to strokes of taper limbs.

Tea over, all ascend the height,
  Kid-climbers of the slippery steep,
And oilcloth chariots expedite,
  Toboganning the grassy sweep.

I, turning home, espied a child
  Perched on the seat beside my door,
She wore no hat, her hair was wild,
  She had a rumpled pinafore.

A lady said, " This child I found
  Alone among the hills, astray ;
I led her down to safer ground,
  But whence she comes I cannot say.

" Come, can you tell me what's your name ? "
    " I'm Todsie Lewis," she replied.
" And where's the place from which you came ? "
    " In Silver Street," she said, " we bide."

" How old are you, my little maid ?
    " And how came you so far to roam ? "
" Three and a 'alf " was all she said,
    " My Daddy 'll come to fetch me home."

I led her in and entertained,
    Calling the children from their play ;
She drank some milk, but then explained
    "At Mrs. Boyd's I've had my tay."

" At Mrs. Boyd's ! "   Might the police-
    Man know her ?   Here there seemed a clue,
I sought that guardian of the peace,
    He gave no aid,—they seldom do.

Then with the rocking-horse she played,
    And asked, " Whose is this lovely Gee ? "
Pursuing her own thoughts, she said,
    " Who goes along with your bai-bee ? "

She sat and gallopped on her throne,
    Town-bred philosopher of three ;
The situation all her own,
    Devoid of all timidity.

We thought, " What can be done to-night ? "
    When presently the road there crossed
A little girl half-dazed with fright,
    And seekers of a baby lost.

I showed her of her sister safe,
  And took her to the Nursery ;
At last, being found, the little waif,
  Then, not till then, began to cry.

Thus ended all these wild alarms,
  But she did not seem overjoyed ;
I took her gently in my arms,
  And gave her back to Mrs. Boyd,

Who cried, " For shame !   Where *have* you been ? "
  Yet took her not unkindly back.
I spared to say, " You should have seen ! "
  In hopes she'd spare the intended smack !

A WESTMORELAND COUNTRY HOUSE, 1898.

DEAR mansion in the rolling North,
 Whose clouds your heathery mountains fleck,
From larch-clad gables peering forth
 Above the rock-encircled beck.

I love thy glorious solitude,
 Six miles from anywhere on earth,
How uplands bare and climate shrewd
 Increase thy charm of inward worth!

Of those I love, the yearly home,
 Whence often with a strengthened heart
But feet reluctant thence to roam,
 I've turned, of toil to bear my part.

Back to this August trysting-place
 Meet year by year a cheery band,
With bronzed or wan or care-worn face,
 From Bank and Bar and Foreign strand ;

Remembered once as slips of boys,
 Dissemblers of the hour mis-spent,
And wooers of tempestuous noise,
 Engrossing oft translations lent.

  I taught them once, they teach me still,
   Bearing the fruit I tried to sow,
  For these have thews to breast the hill,
   I'm fain to guard the butt that's low,

Content, while braver fusiliers
   Confront point-blank the ascending pack,
If I can rake the wing that veers
   Past the tall heather down the slack.

Dear friends! They all can tell me much,
   Each in his line, of that and this,
They stop the cocks I cannot touch,
   They score the cannons that I miss.

We pass : and more than one loved form
   Has gone from sight beyond the veil,
Yet still the hearth and hearts are warm,
   And nothing breaks love's sweet entail.

New generations overlap
   The tide-marks that the last has left,
New trees replace with fresher sap
   Old foliage ere of grace bereft,

Though one no longer walks the fells,
   And one is rarer than we would,
And one has heard the marriage bells,
   And for the better left the good.

Press we to gain the higher range
   As conscious of our mortal doom ;
What harm, though, as we climb, we change
   For ptarmigan the grouse's plume ?

TO S. A. D.

FAREWELL TO DUNSKEY.
Aug. 5th, 1894.

GAIUS, my single-hearted host,
   Or rather with old Mnason paired,
Seeking your glorious Northern coast
   To act the hospitable laird !

Accept these thanks for healthful rest
   And welcome bright, from one who passed
But freshly, a belated guest,
   With swelling midriff, to Belfast.

Revolving much of those he found,
   Keen spendthrifts of a month's inside,
Who in their daily toilsome round
   Stand bravely battling with the tide.

Heroes of workmen's lecture halls,
   From Oxford House and Hackney Wick,
Here smite discurrent billiard balls
   And breathless hang upon the click :

Get up at nine, or haply ten,
   Bear-fight, and chaff, and jest, and shout,
And, fishers otherwhile of men,
   Enraptured land the twelve-ounce trout.

They track the grouse, o'er rabbits glower,
   These men of works and faith so ripe,
Long for the sacred luncheon-hour,
   Then fumble for the holier pipe.

These queenly dames whose grace enchants
   With classic robe and auburn tress,
Tend factory-girls in vulgar haunts,
   Loud-toned, I fear, of louder dress!

Head Masters of Olympian mien
   Here find repose from every ill,
One leaves the doctor's cocáine
   For anæsthetics of the hill.

My Lady of protecting eyes
   Lest thee or him should ill befall
Watches with new anxieties,—
   Rufus not closelier joined with Paul.

Musicians famed through Europe wide,
   Whose ears no choirs may satisfy,
Patient, yet wincing, here abide
   The Kirk's discordant psalmody.

From one, whose ever trenchant wit
   Nor wounds, nor ever fails to score,
His lamp at Ruskin's altar lit,
   The moralist of breakfast lore,

We learn how glass should not be bright,
   Why napkins soiled are best to use ;
He knows each flower, he scans each height,
   He paints dame Nature's rarest hues ;

Rails at tobacco, says he'll bathe,
   Gets up his Plautus for next Half,
(His neck artistic ties enswathe,)
   Evokes, yet scorns, the inspiring laugh.

We go.   Yet while we turn away,
  Leave something of our hearts behind,
And bid the breezes of Dunskey
  Strengthen thy body, cheer thy mind.

May grouse, with numbers bolder grown
  Less nervously avoid their fate,
Old Cameron 'neath the burden groan,
  —No ill-timed jokes on holding straight

Deem that thy good is others' wealth,
  No shame, to be by friends gainsaid ;
And quaff to the Lord Abbot's health
  Flagons of home-brewed lemonade.

While I who live by laxer laws,
  From maxims which I most revere
Seek refuge in a conscience-clause,
  And ' vert ' like a Gladstonian Peer

CARMEN SCHOLARE.

(Past and Present.)

Set to Music by Sir Walter Parratt.

COME, listen, Etonians, great and small,
 To a sound patriotic song,
And shake the old roof of the College Hall
 With a chorus to rouse Hong-Kong !
Let the Tenors and Basses all keep their places,
 And hit the note true and square,
With the Altos backing, whose voices are cracking,
 While the rest of you sing the air.

> CHORUS.—Not all to be sharp and clever,
> Is the summit of our endeavour,
> But our lives to bend
> To the nobler end
> Is the glory of Eton ever !

'Tis twelve full weeks since our opening date,
 But they've gone with an arrow's flight,
We had most of us gone up a stone in weight
 And an inch and a half in height.
The new Sixth Form looked so fresh and nice
 As in stickups they all appeared,
And the weekly shave would no more suffice
 To keep down the growing beard.

> CHORUS.—Not all to be sharp, &c.

But now the old Half it is nearly beat,
    And summer's a far off dream,
And the House Cup waits, like a maiden sweet
    To be won by the bravest team !
Then play up, all, never yield one point,
    Play up as Etonians should :
There's Elliman's Oil for the wounded joint,
    If it fails, there is Wharton Hood !

   Chorus.—Not all to be sharp, &c.

They say we are changed from the good old days,
    Grown softer and fonder of ease :
And soon we shall hear the old tales that amaze,
    From Colonels and bald J. P.'s :
When the coverts are shot, and the logs glow red,
    And they talk of the times of yore,
And the well-worn eloquence gets its head
    From the Governor's " Thirty-four ! "

   Chorus.—Not all to be sharp, &c.

And have we not read it in Maxwell Lyte,
    And learnt at our grandsire's feet,
How their Dames would call them at dead of night,
    To rise and be flogged by Keate ?
How they poached the pheasants in Windsor Park
    Or ever the dawn grew red,
And were back by six to school in the dark
    With never a thought of bed ?

   Chorus.—Not all to be sharp, &c.

They had no " Trials," those grand old boys,
    They worked for pure learning's thirst,
They went to Oxford and made some noise,
    For each got his double First !
They cared not a rush for the Irish Vote,
    They recked not a rap for France ;
They sat on the Russians, they sat in the Boat,
    And the Harrow boys had no chance !

       CHORUS.—Not all to be sharp, &c.

Yet we too are chips from the old Block reft,
    And where Eton demands our powers,
We can break the record our fathers left,
    May our sons in their turn break ours !
Our bowlers can " york," and our Eights can " slide,"
    And when England has need of men,
We think we shall know whither Honour must guide,
    As well as they knew it then !

       CHORUS.—Not all to be sharp, &c.

Our School, though the Fates cut short each yarn,
    Moves onward a deathless line ;
Hereafter, as Parry excels old Arne,
    Some treble may both outshine !
When Roberts is perched with Wellington,
    When Balfour is paired with Pitt,
The busts of our worthies may well gaze down
    On grandsons who've got some grit !

       CHORUS.—Not all to be sharp, &c.

While the Royal Flag on the Castle floats,
    While Eton has glorious fame,
We won't sell our conscience, nor turn our coats,
    Nor do what we once held shame.
The task that surpasses the wit of man,
    We'll leave without further fuss ;
We'll be proud of our School, and do what we can
    That the School may be proud of us !

      CHORUS.—Not all to be sharp, &c.

GRAVIORA.

THE CENTURY'S ANTE-FINAL.
(For the Chief Musician.)

RESPLENDENT beams are kindling in the East.
Awake, ye nations, to a nobler day!
From port to port, from spire to spire, the ray
Illumines commerce freed and powers released.
—Ye, guests erewhile at England's Royal Feast,
Pass friend to friend along the Atlantic breeze:
Join heart with heart, while threads that knit the seas
Flash love, and joy in brotherhood increased!
So be the time remembered in the close
And sunset of this Age, which ebbs amain.
But thou, O Sovereign, may'st thou long sustain
That burden which thy people's love bestows,
The burden of a rule so richly blest,
Of England's Reigns the longest, and the best!

IN CONFIRMATIONEM FILIAE
C. B. J.

CELIA celata florens contenta juventa,
　　Nota puellari sedulitate domi,
Musarum cultrix, fugientis avarior horae,
　　Cara patri, matrem nata referre tuis,
Stes firmata Fide : Crucis indefessa satelles,
　　Sis memor ereptae, sis superantis amans,
Et cum sera aderit, nec non optabilis hora,
　　Celia caelicolis sis mea juncta choris.

Etonae, Id. Martiis,
A. S. MDCCCLXXXVIII.

TO L. S. J.
On her Confirmation.

LILIANA, liliorum nuncupata nomine,
  Instar arboris, sed annos nata vix septendecim,
Floris ut proceritatem, sic reponas gratiam,
Apta Virginis Beatae quae feras insignia.
Quae, sonos Annuntiantis ut recepit Angeli,
Liliorum suavitatem porrigentis dexterâ,
Continens utrâque palmâ praescios Dei sinus,
Leniter demissa voltum, Canticum illud nobile
Fertur edixisse, tantas nec vices expalluit.
Tuque confirmata Sancti Spiritus praesentiâ,
Sanctitate, caritate, gratiâ, constantiâ,
Fortis esto, sic futuris par eris laboribus,
Par patris secunda votis augurantis omina.

ON A WINDOW IN THE LOWER CHAPEL, REPRESENTING MARTHA AND MARY.

(In Memoriam A. Agar.)

YE stand in light, ye sisters twain,
    Marked by your Lord as emblems apt,
Martha, of zeal to entertain,
    Mary, of contemplation rapt.

Yet I would deem that each one shared
    The virtues of her sister sweet,
That Mary oft the meal prepared
    While Martha listened at the Feet.

And she of the devoted heart,
    I think, for worship was more free,
More blest to chose the holier part
    Through Martha's deft housewifery.

And surely Christ spoke not in scorn,
    Who graciously partook that food.
Intolerance He would gently warn,
    But not deny both parts were good.

While we whose needs are human, miss
    The loss of those who were our gain,
Who sacrificed the higher bliss
    And acquiesced in cares mundane.

Some few we gaze on wonderingly,
    Who perfectly the two combine,
Pointing to higher mystery,
    The human blent with the divine.

St. Edward's, Kidderminster.

[*An Albatross was found dead on the sea-shore in Australia with a silver band round its neck, covering a message to the effect that thirteen men had been for some months cast away on the Crozet Islands.*]

HOW long ere thou didst light,
    Brave bird, in urgent flight
Sweeping the pathless deserts of the sea?
    Not now to sport at will,
    With wings outstretched and still,
    Circling some bark as formerly
To keep the seamen joyous company.

    Those mystic laws that bind
    Thy race to human kind
Laid on thee strong compulsion forth to fare,
    Forth from those Crozet isles,
    On for three thousand miles,
    If thou mightst rescue from despair
Those dozen shipwrecked souls who linger there ;

    That piteous message found
    Among thy plumage bound
Where on thy neck the silver collar shone ;
    —Struggling but just to reach
    The far Australian beach,
    And English eyes that watch thereon,
Then die exhausted, but thy mission done.

Sure not without His call,
Who marks the sparrow's fall,
And knows the worthiness of every loss ;
A mystic sacrifice
Of human lives the price,
Thou liest stretched beneath the Southern Cross,
Friend of our kind, devoted Albatross.

TO HER MAJESTY WILHELMINA, QUEEN OF THE NETHERLANDS. 1898.

SWEET Maiden-Monarch, o'er thy shallow sea
   We too would join thy country's glad acclaim :
We too can raise a heartfelt prayer for thee,
   For England knows the glories of thy name.

And we have felt what worth a nation gains
   When such as thou shalt be ascends its throne,
What loyalties encircle her who reigns
   In virtue o'er a people like thine own.

" All things wherein small peoples may be great."
   This was thy noble, thy ennobling, call.
Such be thy policy, thy cares of state.
   God save from aught which makes great peoples small !

" Orange for Holland ne'er enough can do."
   So thy brave voice rang out in accents clear.
What marvel that men wept ?   Be Holland true !
   Eyes that wept then should shed no baser tear.

Sole but sufficient Scion of thy Line,
   Strong is thy Throne, deep founded on the past :
But deeper founded on those hearts of thine ;
   Not back, but forward, be the eyes now cast.

So shall the Remnant-Branch again take root
   Downward, while sweetly blooms the Orange Flower,
And for the dawning century bear fruit
   Upward, refulgent with its golden dower.

Long may'st thou reign by loving hearts adored,
   Queen of thy prospering folk : nor only so,
But Mother like thy Mother, till thy Lord
   Call thee to higher crowns than these below.

DISCESSURUS.

TO THE EDITOR OF THE "TIMBRALLS CHRONICLE," IN ANSWER TO KIND VERSES LAMENTING OUR DEPARTURE.

THERE'S sorrow in all parting, yet some light
  And comfort comes in thinking those we knew
Will feel some pang of pain.   Can this be right?
  I know not, only knowing it is true.

No, it is not all selfishness ; we nurse
  The obvious, but the deeper sense we leave.
We would not be forgotten, but 'twere worse,
  If you for us could permanently grieve.

Eton can tolerate no vacant place.
  The ranks close up, soon we are missed no more.
Apply one patch, and in the dizzy race
  The punctured tyre runs even as before.

So, for all that sweet sorrow you bestow,
  And verse all sobbing with uneven fret,
Your faces shall again with pleasure glow,
  And silvery laughter wake the glad quartette.

Dear happy group : beyond all others blest
  In charm and sympathy and parents' love,
A school within a home, within your nest
  Culling that profit for which others rove :

Cleave to your games, your music, and your arts.
  Fate brings not yet on us that sadder time.
To lose you is unthinkable,—true hearts
  Belie not so the promise of their prime.

Eton, 1898.   ι.

.

THE MARTIAN.

WHAT, Grimston? Weakly Prose forgot again?
Will nothing clear that problematic brain
Of Conics, Cosines, and Chimaeras Dyer?
Well, we'll have Verse this week then!—Blink not so,
But mount thy Pegasus, or,—if that flyer
Won't rise with 18 stone,—thy stoutest shire!
Behemoth paws the ground!—You cannot rhyme?
I'll help you then,—it won't be the first time!

Where were ye, Nymphs of Harrow, on that night
When Grimston came to Eton? On the height
Named of the Primrose?—or 'neath Ducker's Pool,
That he was suffered to desert your School?
The leech laid down point blank, "Not on that Hill!
"The air's too bracing. He'll be always ill!"
"Let Eton have the lad," sighed sainted Bob,
"He's beetle-blind, and cannot play a lob!
"Exchange looks well. Two colts are worth a screw;
"V. E.'s got down young Studd,—young Dowson too!"
"Good," cried the Earl: "To Eton he shall go,
"I'll write to Arthur James.—They'll make him row!"

Thus didst thou come, as dropt on earth from Mars,
Big, flaxen-haired, a wastrel from the stars:
—Oft lost among them. I can see thee now,
Poring o'er Euclid with reflective brow,
Mild-eyed and sympathetic, oft alone,
Heedful for others, heedless of thine own:

Meek, unresentful, unobtrusive, shy,
Quite un-fourth-formed, sat upon easily
By rougher natures, to thy fellows kind,
Loving thy Beethoven, of tastes refined.
One marked thee buy caged linnets from a lout
For sixpences, to let them all fly out.
A nature labelled " Fragile," " Glass with care ! "
And " This side up," with predilection rare
For Measles, Mumps, and ailments more than Job's ;
The fated feeding-ground for fell microbes.
But youth and good surroundings gained the day :
These passed,—but Mathematics came to stay !

The years rolled on.   Behold the Lower Boy
Grown big, his soul yet guiltless of alloy.
Like some white ox from pure Clitumnus' mead,
Straight-backed, the choicest of Mevania's breed,
Soft-eyed, broad-muzzled, patient of the yoke,
Meet for a child to sit on, guide, and stroke.
He skilled to find the circle's centre C,
But not his skiff's centre of gravity.
The force, the scull, the rowlock, he could sum,
But not his body's equilibrium.
When he went out, Old Thames South Meadow laved,
When he went down, its depths his pebbles paved,
And wondering dredgers would fish up, by dives,
Gold spectacles with prehistoric knives !
Still, propped by others, he could ply an oar,
And rowed to victory his House's Four,
Yet wore scug coats though in the Boats he sat,
And almost beat his Tutor's shocking hat !

The scene is changed.   A chief among the rest
Behold him now, of habits self-possessed,
The pride of Pop, five in the Eton Eight,
Winning victorious the Ladies' Plate.
On Martian Kalends, (there were some to laugh)
He acts High Admiral,—his first Lent Half!
And on the Brocas holds promotion's key,
The loyal viceroy of an absentee.
See him in Chapel, as the Provost nears,
Towering above the pageant of his peers.
Orchid on breast, with orthopaedic throat
And faultless tie,—a Bondsman built that coat!
With mien defiant, gazing up at North,
Hear him declaim his Schiller on the Fourth,
Fire in his glance, a miracle of ease,
Rasping his tonsils for Teutonic G's.

Eton to thee a step-dame kind hath proved,
My Grimston, one well worthy to be loved.
Not least for this, that she hath often taught
Authority to those who never sought,
Enjoining rule on some who least aspired,
Obedience, too, on some who least retired.
And I, too, for thy two years' captaincy
Render thee loving thanks : for harmony
Uninterrupted by the smallest strife.
May these be samples of thy coming life,
My dear White Elephant, thou fated brand
Snatched out of Harrow fire!   And now our band
Breaks rank.   Parade is over, and we stand
Both on the platform's edge—you, bound for Town,
Travel by first-class up, I third-class down.

Happy in this, that since we cannot stay,
We leave together on the self-same day.
I'd not outlive thee, Grimston! At my need,
Captains might follow thee,—but who succeed?

These for thy Verses. Show them up for thine.
Take broadruled quickly,—they're the last I'll sign!

VALETE.

HOW can I pass without a voice of prayer
    And thanks to thee, O Eton, who hast nursed
My youth and manhood with continuous care?
Save that for four short years thou gavest me
To thy more stately Sister, not more fair,
(Queen, thou, of common culture, she, of rare :)
Each offering me her good most lavishly,
The blame be mine, if good by ill reversed!

How much, I know not.   This is no slight weight
Which lies on one that looks across the past,
And sets himself awhile to meditate,
Where much is given, how much will be required ;
How far the output answers to the rate
Of hours allowed, in scale proportionate ;
—Little of all to which he once aspired,
And of that little something, what will last?

Yet here, if anywhere, is given a chance
To build on that Foundation which is laid,
Something whereby good causes may advance,
Something of worth that may not suffer loss,
But stand the fire in mystic tolerance
When boyhood's ardent dreams no more entrance,
When manhood's harder metal turns to dross,
And only that remains which cannot fade.

DISCESSURUS.

Truly a standard arduous to attain.
Yet is not this the test which we must face?
Easy it were, contented to remain
By this fresh tide of youth that keeps us young,
Be led instead of leading, watch the strain
Of other workers, feel the flowery chain
Of happy memories around us hung:
But would this be to merit Eton's grace?

Then I'll put off my arms, and ask to rest.
But you, whose powers are fresh, whose minds are strong,
My comrades erst, and in your service blest,
None faithful more, Oh call me still your friend,
Past Master in the art I once professed,
Sometimes, perhaps, an all too willing guest.
My heart is loyal, and I leave the Great
To join the Greater Eton. Do I wrong?

And you, dear Scholars, whom I hate to fail,
Learn for me one more lesson ere I go.
Value the old, but let the new prevail.
Fresh starts bring more of profit than you dream.
Your House count more than Colours, and the School
More than the House: yet confidently hail
Your Country above both. These colours nail
Unto the mast, and drift not with the stream:
And God protect you from the inner foe!

To you, kind Sirs, who welcome to your door
My storm-tost crew, I venture this to say :
Look on them kindly ; give them of your lore,
Good honest souls, who lean towards your light.
Ask them not perfect.   If they vex you sore,
Lay all you can to their old Tutor's score.
If nought avails you, then write home at night.
—Sleep on your letter though, and burn next day !